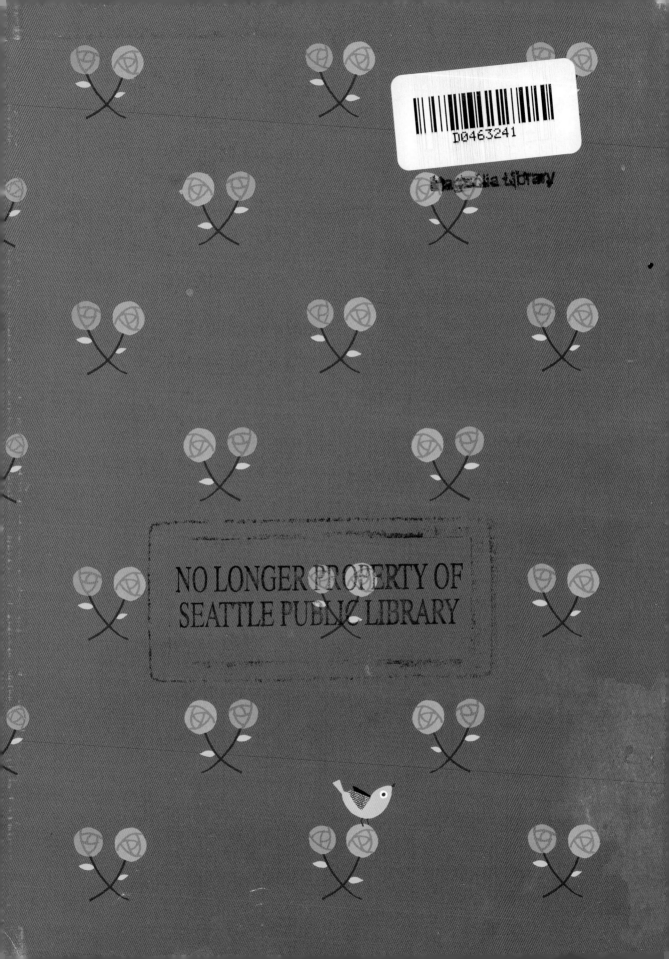

First published in the United States of America in 2016
by Chronicle Books LLC.

Originally published in Italy in 2014 by Kite Edizioni S.r.l.
under the title *Quando un elefante si innamora*.

Library of Congress Cataloging-in-Publication Data available.

ISBN 978-1-4521-4727-7

Manufactured in China.

MIX
Paper from
responsible sources
FSC™ C104723
FSC
www.fsc.org

Typeset in Lunchbox.

10 9 8 7 6 5 4 3 2

Chronicle Books LLC
680 Second Street
San Francisco, CA 94107

Chronicle Books—we see things differently.
Become part of our community at www.chroniclekids.com.

DAVIDE CALI   ALICE LOTTI

WHEN AN ELEPHANT
FALLS IN LOVE

chronicle books · san francisco

When an elephant falls in love,
he does many foolish things.

He hides whenever he sees her.

He takes a bath every day, and
even washes behind his ears.

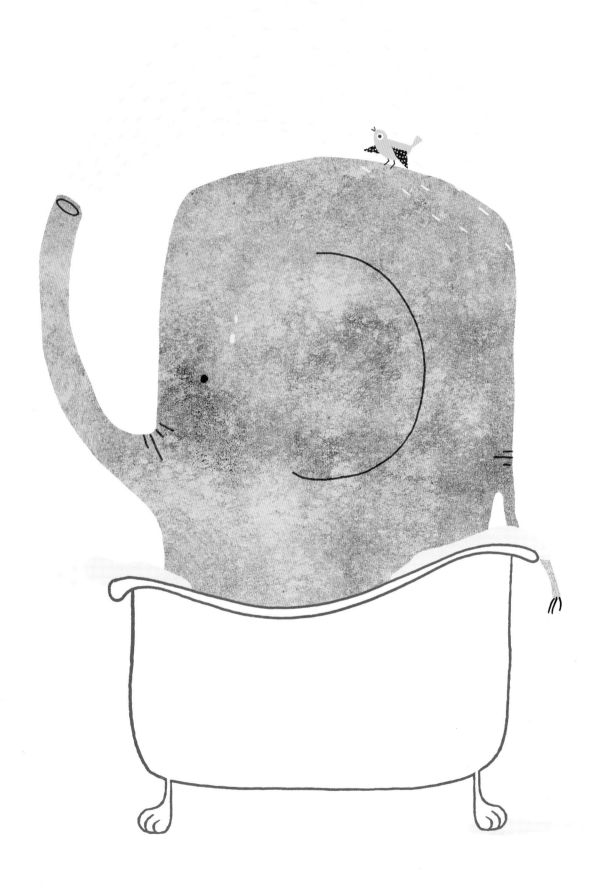

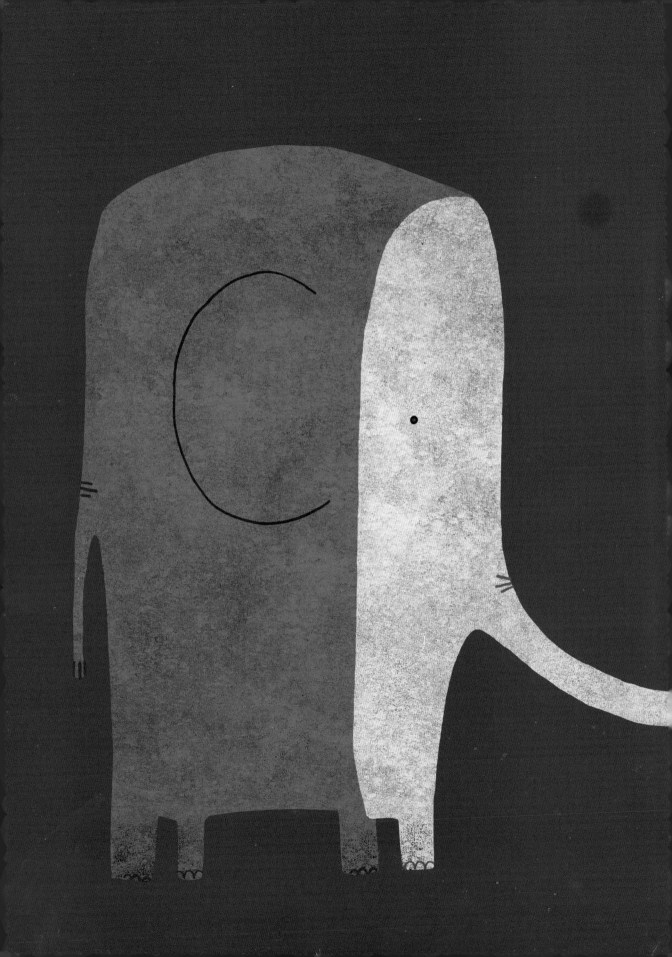

He tries to be healthy, but
ends up finishing the cheesecake.

When an elephant falls in love,
he dresses with care.
But sometimes he just can't decide!

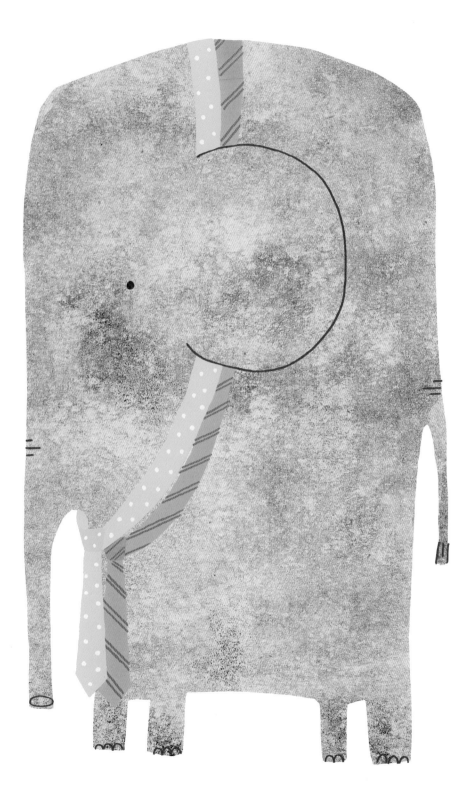

"Maybe something more stylish?"

When an elephant falls in love, he
writes letters that he'll never send.

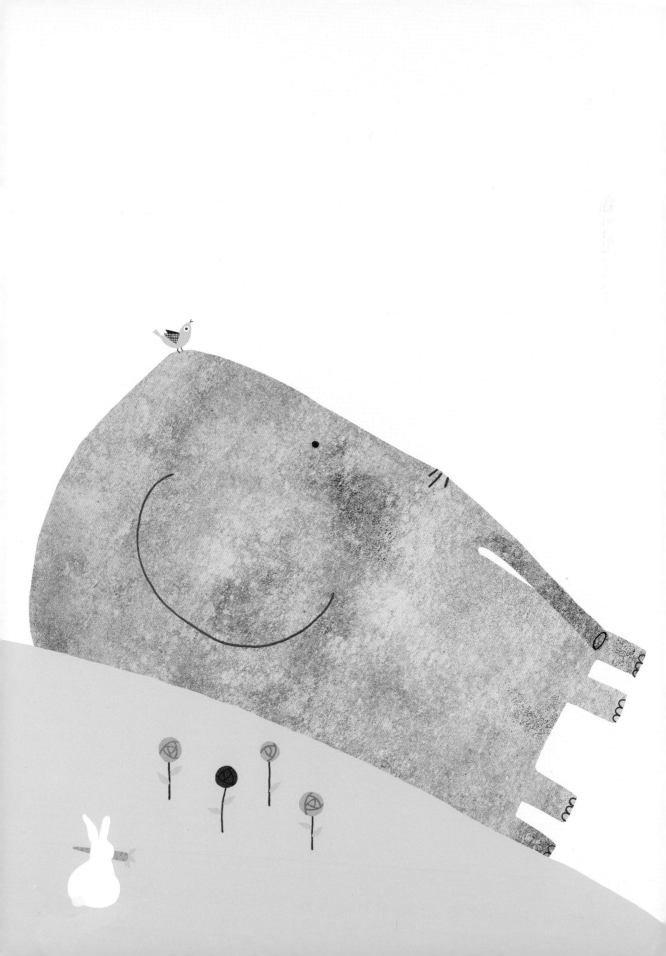

And he stares at the clouds for hours and hours.

When an elephant falls in love,
he leaves flowers at her door.

But he runs away after ringing the bell.

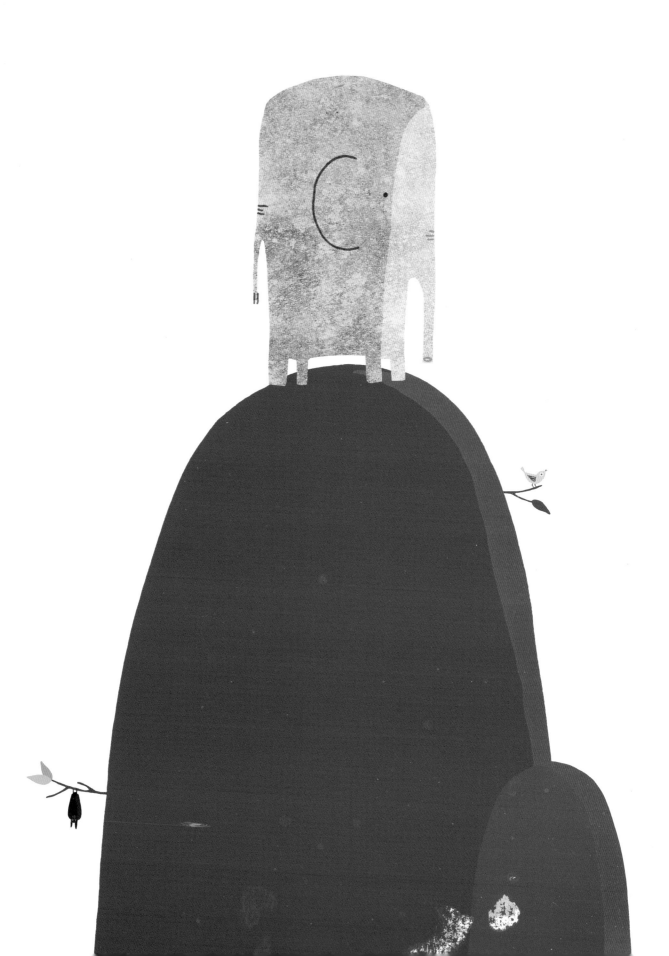

When an elephant falls in
love, sometimes he's sad.

"If only she knew I existed!"

Until, one day . . .
"Who is it?"

Could it be . . . ?

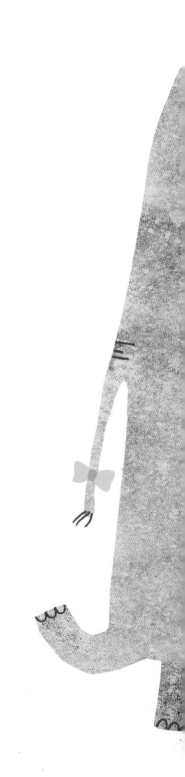

It's love!

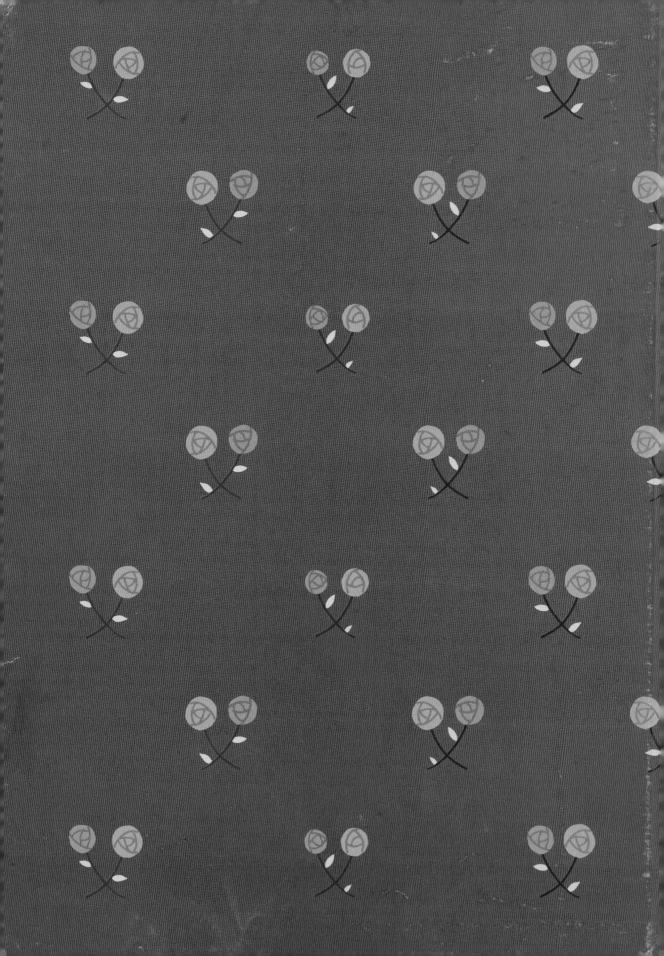